MW00975350

# Beyond
# Hocus-Pocus
## by CHRIS BLAINE

*Chris Blaine*

Second Printing
1,000 copies

copyright September 1997
TXU832-012
Chris Blaine

Barnett Educational Supplies, Inc.
P.O. Box 22626
Savannah, Georgia 31403-2626

## ACKNOWLEDGEMENT

Some of the stories to follow were spontaneous, imaginative creations at a campfire setting. For some reason the audience of youngsters and adults were of the impression the stories were of a read-and-recite origin. When told that they were, for the most part, inventions, many suggested that they should be recorded. As you might suspect, some of the stories are true. The youngsters asked time-and-again to hear a few of the same stories until, as time passed, each became a legend. New kids to the campfire circle would beg to hear the stories for the first time.

This booklet is dedicated to my son, Kirk, who got me to the campfire and to my wife, Sally, who is my chief critic and editor.

Illustrations are by Tom Tretter, Ian Shickle, and Kevin Thomas, who are respectively a Savannah School Of Art and Design graduate, student, and faculty member.

Any profit from the sale of this booklet are to be donated to a youth organization.

Loves criminal conjure abides

Lost to faces where no warmth resides;

But striking at the daily calendar glow

Shortening the program that goes to slow;

And groping for sands long lost to man,

And tilling memories of barren ghost lands,

And compiling a thought of all life span,

Then goaling away with fire and fan.

So lost to faces which no warmth revives

Loves criminal conjure still survives.

# TABLE OF CONTENTS

# NOUS VIVIONS A JAMAIS

In Roman mythology, Venus, the goddess of love, commanded her son, Cupid, to make Psyche, the most beautiful princess in the world, to fall in love with the ugliest man in the world. When Cupid met Psyche, he fell in love with the princess at first sight. Cupid visited her in the dark of night pretending that he was the ugliest man. He hid her in a remote place thinking that his mother would not discover the ruse. He eventually was discovered when Psyche and Venus lit a candle as he slept. Venus condemned both to wander the world apart searching in the darkness for each other. Hence was born the word, Psyche, used today to describe the inner thoughts of the mind.

The psyche is again tested in the Egyptian Book of the Dead. Upon the death of a Pharaoh, he had to visit the high priest in various temples along the banks of the Nile River. To accomplish the month-long journey by barge, his body had to be embalmed. Otherwise his body would putrefy before all the ceremonies and oaths could be administered. Forty-five responses to commandments had to be rendered favorably before his body and spirit could become immortal. It was from this beginning 3,000 years before Christ that the body and psyche were viewed as two distinct parts of life.

Sigmond Freud distinguished three levels of Psyche: the Id, the Ego, and the Super Ego. These are the spirits that inhabit the mind. The Id is the primal instinct or urge to perpetuate itself. Air, food, water, and other basic drives for pleasure are motivating forces. The Ego is the defense mechanism, or simply put, the excuse that we give for not doing what we expect of ourselves. The Super Ego controls the Ego and Id by setting up standards from which shame and guilt grow when the Id and Ego are out of balance.

Normally each Psyche spirit is delicately balanced, one against the other, but function in unison. Think of the cogged wheel in a machine turning against other cogged wheels of different size, speeds, and durations. Each has a

1

different function but they all touch each other periodically or perpetually to obtain the purpose of the machine - a machine such as a clock.

Rene' Descartes was a mathematician. He is considered the father of analytical geometry because of his "Rule of Signs" which determined the value of roots in equations. He applied his mathematical genius into the study of philosophy, more particularly into the area of the psychic phenomenon that separates the spirit from the body.

Rene' described in a publication that he was able to disassociate his mind from his body. He could watch his body from a corner of his bedroom as it slept. He could travel in the dark, liberated from his body. He had to return to his body before it woke or his body would die without its soul. His contemporaries ridiculed him because he failed to prove to anyone that he could mind-travel. He never divulged his secret method employed to achieve this feat. In his long lost journals discovered by a graduate student at the University of Paris, he finally stated in the closing pages that his body was old, tired, and in need of rest. He planed to leave his body for dead and invade a younger, more healthy body while it slept. He felt that his Super Ego was sufficiently strong enough to dominate that of his host. He would become the spirit that possessed a body.

He recognized that he would have to gently fit his cogged wheels into place so that aberrant behavior would not be recognized by others. More importantly, he wanted to continue his work and leave an enduring legacy for others. His body died in the year 1650. On his grave marker were inscribed the words: "NOUS VIVIONS A JAMAIS".

Translated they mean: I WILL LIVE FOREVER. To prove that he had in fact achieved eternal life, he recorded in his journal that he would make his host scratch the letter "R" on the back of the headstone and every place that he slept. The graduate student verified the mark of "R". Rene' got the last laugh on his contemporaries who thought him a fool.

Nightly, the letter "R" might be smeared on a bathroom mirror with a bar soap, might be scratched in the dirt beside a campfire, or might be written in the dew on a car windshield. Those, who know of this story, will recognize the sign; others, who do not know of the significance of the sign, will not.

# GRIFFIN

In the 1960's a medicine was developed by a well-known and reputable pharmaceutical company that helped people with digestion and nausea. It passed testing by the Food and Drug Administration and was widely prescribed by physicians to help people with weak or spastic stomachs.

The Food and Drug Administration did not do a long range test using Thalidomide on woman who had recently conceived while using the medication. Through this oversight, numerous babies were born with flagrant defects such as too many or too few fingers, hands, and arms. These were just some of the obvious defects. Beneath the skin were incredible deformities such as multiple or missing organs. Most were still-born wads of lumpy flesh with distorted skeletal and muscular systems. Some were so deformed that only by finding an eye or mouth could you tell top from bottom. It was nearly impossible to communicate with one that did survive birth. They had a language all their own - much like frogs, snakes, cats, insects, and birds. To some degree, all of these mentioned creatures would make up one animal.

First. Let me tell you about the abnormalities that took place in the medieval times when witches brewed potions and cast spells. There were creatures that were half-horse and half-man; they were called Centurions. There were lizards larger than the Monitors found in the South Sea Islands. They were called Dragons. Every time that one was destroyed, the church would raise a statue in its likeness called a Gargoyle.

Second. Around the time of the birth of Christ, there were extraordinary celestial activities. I am sure that you know of the star that shone brightly in the sky that guided the Wisemen to baby Jesus. There were also enormous sun spots which are known to produce Alpha, Beta, and Omega particles. These particles are just like X-Ray - they are so small that they can pass right through the body without

5

making a hole, or at least it is almost impossible to find one. Every now and then one collides with the chromosomes in a human female's egg. Something is destroyed, erased, or altered; we don't know which or what. One of the most obvious mutations is the Albino. Let me say that in the realm of mutations, this one is mild. Think about the thousands that you don't see.

Finally. When you combine vigorous sun spot activity, Thalidomide, potions and spells in a clinical environment, which can concentrate all these forces into an outcome that is not haphazard but fact certain, then you can create some real monsters. That is just what happened about twenty years ago in a private clinic outside of Savannah.

Dr. Horowitz had been censored by the American Medical Association for his bazaar experiments within his high-walled compound on Alligator Island. They finally revoked his license to practice medicine when a few of Dr. Horowitz's animals got beyond the electrified, razor-wired fence and over the wall. They ravaged the island before being shot or trapped. But a few never were recovered. Some people rationalized that they had drowned and were eaten by the alligators or sharks. Dr. Horowitz died in the fire started by the town's people who were outraged and panicked by the appearance of a Griffin that had perched itself on the steeple of the Baptist Church on Sunday morning. His entire compound was burned to the ground along with most of his creatures and journals.

There are still some around, or so I have been told. Every now and then, when everybody thinks that it is safe to go outside at night, a steer will be ripped apart and half eaten. Weird tracks are found in the sand and an odor that is repulsive lingers for days. It stirs up the mosquitoes and loves to hide in the mossy places. It feeds in the dark.

# GREEN-EYED LADY

One this same day in 1979, a family of four was sidelined on Interstate I-16 with car trouble. The car may have overheated or may have run out of gas; but in any event, the old Chevy Caprice Classic was a constant source of aggravation to the Pendletons. It seemed to have a mind of its own - running and not running of its own free will. Mr. Pendleton was always under the hood trying to coax a few more miles out of the tired old car. It was so reluctant to give more in the combat of who had the strongest will. All in all, Mr. Pendleton probably spent as much time in making repairs and in money buying parts as it took to originally build the car.

His wife Thelma always reminded him of this, "Someday this car, with us in it, will die on I-16 out in the middle of nowhere. Then what are we going to do?", she would say. If she only knew what would happen, she might have been a nicer person.

George's shoulders bent inward a little more each day. His eyes never looked up. She made him feel so inferior. His job in the maintenance department at the paper mill was just as demeaning. George was known at the plant as "Geet" because everybody would yell at George and say, "Geet mow stuff".

The two blue-eyed, blond-haired children were the single source of pride and joy to Thelma. Like little boys, they were bad, but bad in a nice way. They didn't always immediately clean their room or eat every last green bean off their plate. She loved them dearly and tried to spoil them rotten.

When at last the car did die on I-16, Thelma and George stepped out of the car. Thelma's mouth was going a mile-a-minute in a constant barrage of insults to George, his abilities, his family, his ineptness, his incompetence, his manliness. She even turned and kicked the old car in disgust. She gave him everything she had while he buried himself under the hood with his flashlight and tools.

9

George was honestly doing his very best to be a good father to his children and husband to his wife. At the plant he was efficient, good natured, and talented at nursing the old equipment into running through one more shift. George came from a poor white-trash family that wandered like cats. He wasn't sure who his father was or who his brothers and sisters were. George had no education and was only barely able to read and write. On pay day George would unusually get drunk in his car outside of Lucy's Bar & Grill and sleep it off in the driveway of Tillson's Pharmacy. John Tillson would always tap on the window of the Caprice on Saturday morning and tell George it was time to go home.

When the 18-wheeler collided with the Caprice, it almost nearly ran over it. The Caprice was dragged under the tractor tailor for nearly a quarter of a mile before coming to a stop by the Ogeecheee River bridge. The Caprice was so mangled that it could not be recognized as anything built by Chevrolet. The bodies of the two children and George had to be cut out of the twisted and crushed metal box. The three died instantly and, as good souls go, went directly to Heaven.

Thelma, on the other hand, had been knocked unconscious and thrown twenty-three feet down the embankment and into the underbrush along the river bank. She laid there through the flashing lights of the State Patrol and the wrecker. She laid there three hours after everybody had resumed their normal lives.

When she woke, she was totally disoriented. The first words out of her mouth were ones cursing George. She ached all over as she followed a path which led to a dirt road and to an abandoned house that was sometimes used as a hunting lodge when the deer season was in full swing. There were a few canned supplies, and wood and water nearby. She spent most of the next several days in delirium crying for her children and sobbing with pain. She developed a raging fever and began to pass blood in her urine and stool. Her insides were ruptured when she was knocked down the embankment. She was dying a slow, agonizing death that had been George's secret wish. She swore to get even with him as soon as she

10

found her children.

There was no missing person report filed with police. Her body was moved months later to a paupers grave. Nobody was able to connect her severely decomposed body with the bodies of a man and two children as being from the same family. Consequently, they were buried in separate graves, in separate cemeteries, on opposite sides of the city. The after-life spirits never connected.

Her spirit never found peace. During the day she evaporates. But at night near the anniversary of the sudden death of her children, she can be heard moaning, crying, and calling for her children and cursing George. Her ghost wanders back and forth from the house to the river bank, calling for her children between painful sobs. Occasionally, a passing fishing boat has reported seeing something strange along the Ogeechee River bank late while they night-fish.

Her ghost was discovered by two kids camping there three years ago. One heard the noises and went into the cabin at night to investigate. He had been in and out of the cabin all day and was totally unprepared for what would greet him. His sight was totally and permanently blinded after he looked at her face and saw shafts of green light shinning on him from her eyes. He became disoriented and lost in the cabin. He called for his friend to save his life, "Help me! Please help me! I can't get out! Help me get out but don't look at the Green-eyed Lady's face!"

Now for you that think this story is just made up to scare you, then let me remind you that ghosts are real. Do you believe in the Holy Ghost? There are most certainly ghosts good and evil.

If by chance you happen to enter this or any abandoned home place, let me remind you that it is abandoned for a reason. The reason is usually because nobody wanted to live there. Be wary of unsettled spirits that may inhabit old places. I can only imagine what would happen if the Green-Eyed lady mistook one of you for her own child or husband.

# CLICK-CLICK

Many years ago a man was indicted for a brutal murder of a child. The situation was so unusual that I was called into the investigation to testify before the Grand Jury as an expert witness and again to testify later in his very highly publicized trial.

My first love and early career interest was generated from an insatiable fascination with bazaar and macabre crime. I would inject myself into the mind of the perpetrator. I would crawl around dissecting every little fact of early childhood history, relationships with parents and siblings, and environmental stimulation. I would connect these facts into a pattern that would lend itself as a plausible explanation for the predisposition that created, motivated, and satisfied the criminal mind. I had a Ph.D. in the field of Psychology with my major area of study concentration in the field of abnormal behavior. I opened a clinic. My practice gradually became limited to the investigation and therapy of the criminally insane. I was employed by the Defense and prosecuting attorneys for the content of my psychological profiles. My work was very interesting and rewarding. A couple of years ago I retired.

For purposes of confidentially, I will not name the main individual character of this story or his location. Let me just say that his home was not far from this place. In fact it would be about a hour to briskly walk through the woods. He became known as Click-Click. You will know why he got this name as I get further into the story.

The more that I interviewed him, the more I became convinced that he was just as normal as you or I, or at least it was that way in the beginning. What happened to him could have happened to any of us. It probably has, or it probably will. There is a difference between him and us. We know when to stop. He didn't.

It all started, as related to me from his jail cell, when he inadvertently cut his finger with a very sharp ordinary

13

kitchen knife as he was peeling an apple. Sure it was stupid and clumsy, but it happens every day to thousands of people. Each of us has cut ourselves at one time or other. If you haven't, some day you will. Like many of us, he stuck his bleeding finger into his mouth. This by itself was a very natural response. It gave him immediate comfort but it would become a problem later.

He was an educated man with a degree from a northern state university. Again I am limited by confidentially in telling you exactly where. As a student there, he joined no clubs or fraternities, but preferred to be a loner. He kept to himself and virtually had no friends or family to speak of. Although he was intellectual and did well with his studies, he did not draw attention by being the most superlative student. This would have frightened his timid nature to be in the spotlight.

As a young child, his parents pretty much ignored him. He was always good, tidy, clean. He ate his vegetables and never complained or asked for anything for himself. There was no sign of the abnormal rage that was growing inside of him. He always seemed cool, calm and collected. But so is a sleeping tiger. His parents were not close to him. They showed very little affection or notice for him except on the occasion of his birthday. They had their own busy life that pulled they away from home. He had sitters that came for nights, then lasted for weeks. They were on the phone or watching television programs that were of no interest to him. His parents wouldn't waste their money by buying him his own TV set to keep in his room. There was no computer or video game to occupy his time. He was always told, "Go to your room and find a book to read." His thoughts became his friends and family. To be perfectly honest, his parents really didn't want to have children. He had been a mistake.

While at the university, his compulsive thoughts overwhelmed his behavior. He was cutting himself intentionally and licking his own blood. He had scars all over his hands and arms. Some were nasty red welts where they had become infected from contact from bacteria in his saliva or from that old kitchen knife he still used. He always kept his hands in his pockets and wore long sleeved shirts to keep himself hidden.

It was only after he ran out of good skin to cut that he began to buy and eat raw meat. He especially loved to tip the corner of the container where the blood would accumulate into his mouth. This was good but not as good as his own body temperature blood. Suddenly one day he had a vision.

He went to an abattoir or slaughterhouse in the industrial district of the city and was able to purchase a cup of fresh blood. He became a regular visitor and would sit nervously in his 1979 yellow Ford Pinto until he could see the animals to be slaughtered for the day move forward in the holding shoot or could hear the sound of the .22 caliber shot fired into the skull of the first animal. He would stand at the window and watch as the subsequent shot was fired. Hooks were run through the rear heel tendons and the animal was hoisted up and in line on a conveyor belt. As the heart surrendered it's last few beats, the knife-man would slit the jugular vein on the animal's neck. Watching the blood squirt made his mouth water. He shook with the excited anticipation of the satisfying warm taste. He passed his cup forward to the knife-man and ran to his car to gulp his reward down, licking the last drop from the rim. If he waited too long, the blood would thicken like pudding. He used no seasoning or spice. He would sit in his car until he was satisfied that he would not need to make a second or third trip back again and again as he sometimes did.

He developed a taste for good blood and a destain for poor quality stock. On occasions when he obtained the blood of a weak or sickly animal, he knew instantly that the animal had not been properly cared for. It had been neglected and ignored as he had been. He especially liked the blood taken from the neck of a fat pink pig. It seemed to him that it was of much better quality than that of beef steers.

His first brush with the arm of the law was when he broke into the stockyard. On a weekend when the Abattoir was closed, he had developed a critical need, an obsessively compulsive need for a cup of blood. He had gone through his ritual trying to divert his mind from the taste that his mouth craved by doing stuff, like cleaning house, doing his laundry, cleaning his refrigerator. But he gave in. He cornered a steer in the loading chute and cut its throat just like the knife-man, using his old kitchen knife. The animal twisted, thrashed and kicked as he tried to hold his cup to its neck. He was splashed with the contents of the cup and was squirted by the blood flow. He became so frustrated that he crawled into the pen with the animal and attached himself to the neck of the steer, sucking and licking the blood. He was saturated in blood. When he returned home he was in the process of removing his blood soaked cloths when the police pounded at his door. He expressed his feeling of disappointment in his clumsy attack to the arresting officers.

He spent a few months detention in a mental facility but was not rehabilitated. He reverted back to the mutilating perforations of his arms to extract blood. Again the wounds were kept under shirt sleeves. The ward aids never suspected that his calm and serene behavior was kept in check by an occasional drink from his own flesh.

Upon his release, he returned for his final year at school. He found an apartment on the opposite side of town where nobody suspected that he was the same person as the man the police had found covered in blood. Stray cats and dogs disappeared from the street of the neighborhood. Nobody really noticed what was happening until he was caught climbing over a yard fence down the street. A rather plump dachshund with a non-threatening bark. The animal looked like it could be a nice meal until the owner came outside with a .38 police special and ran him off the premise.

He decided to become a Veterinarian and took a job in a small animal hospital for hands-on training. His favorite activity was the disposal of the sick animals. You can imagine his method. Again he was discovered; and although having broken no law, his employer insisted that he voluntarily confine himself to the mental facility for treatment for a brief time. Again he reverted back to his secret cannibalistic, self-mutilation behavior.

He abruptly checked himself out of the treatment center and moved to a house trailer in a remote coastal city. He hunted and foraged for food in the nearby swamp areas. He left no forwarding address and devoted himself to raising hogs. We all know the why and whatfore.

On one of his expeditions deep into the woods, he came upon a scout camp. He crept stealthily in the woods, kneeling, and occasionally lying on the ground as he observed kids running about the campsite totally oblivious to his presence. He began to wonder what one would taste like. He waited until one wandered outside of the campfire light without a flashlight and close by where he was hiding. The kid was taking a leak when the old kitchen knife found it's mark. The gurgling sound caught the ear of the assistant scoutmaster, who had taken a seat close by the fire in the vicinity from the place vacated by the boy. The assistant called out to the boy. "Are you all right?", he asked. There was no reply, only the sound of slurping and a faint rustling of leaves.

Click-Click was so absorbed in his cannibalism that he was oblivious to the approaching assistant. When the assistant saw what he thought he was seeing, he began to pummel Click-Click vigorously with his hickory stave. He thrashed and whipped him until the walking stick broke. Click-Click was beat to the ground. The assistant stomped on top of him repeatedly until he heard Click-Click's femur bone in his leg loudly snap. The assistant was yelling, screaming for anybody to come help him. He ran back to the fire but all had disappeared in fright. When he returned, Click-Click was gone. He returned to his house trailer where he repaired himself. The bone did not heal properly which caused a distinct limp and a "Click-Click" noise with every step, and hence his nickname.

Eventually, the authorities arrived at Click-Click's trailer with blood hounds howling. Click-Click could not get away. After he was placed in jail, I was summoned for a psychological profile by his defense attorney, who was working on a pro-bono basis. Click-Click served a sentence of thirty-five years and was granted parole last month. He was supposed to check in with his parole officer, but he has not been heard of since his release. We suspect that he is in nearby woods behind a bush or tree or outside your window - watching, waiting.

19

# CELLAR

I really don't mind the occasional garden spider that weaves an architecturally intricate web. It is to be admired. I really don't mind watching the little rolly-pollies scurry for cover when a rotted stick is lifted and they are surprised by the bright sun light. They don't threaten me because I can keep a respectable distance. But the cellar of my grandmother's house is a different story.

Not very long ago we visited my grandmother for Thanksgiving. The smell of the food being prepared in the kitchen was warm and familiar. She and my mother had started very early in the morning before I was out of bed. The kitchen was in total disarray with a clutter of pots, pans, roasters, mixing bowls, and jars with various contents. Food in stages of preparation and kitchen cutlery were scattered on every counter, cooking surface, and table. Both were adorned with pretty bibbed aprons with white ruffles, the badge of a good cook. I knew that the food would have to be excellent because the cooks exchanged a constant dialogue of soothing sounds after each sample taste. Occasionally one would say that it needed a little bit more of some spice that had an unusual name and only added the suspense to the final outcome of their day's labor.

I was the typical little boy of ten who liked to stick a finger for a taste of whatever looked good, ready or not. I must have been a nuisance because they shooed me out of the kitchen area from time to time. "Go outside and play." Grandma would scold. Nothing was more interesting to me than what they were doing. Finally in desperation, Grandma told me, "Go to the cellar for a pint jar of beets." To me this was the final and ultimate kiss of death. There was nothing short of being flung into burning Hell that scared me more, and she knew it.

During the summer months she planted a fairly large vegetable garden in the bottom near the house. She had always had a garden even when there was nobody much

21

around to eat all the jars of food she canned. She had a local negro man who helped her for years with the unspoken agreement that he could have all that he wanted of the harvest to feed his family. He would come either very early in the morning or late in the evening to avoid the heat of the day. I guess maybe he might have had another job, but he was faithful. After Grandpa died, he was about her best friend, although she would never say so. When he was sick once, she picked vegetables and took them to his family. His job was to plow and weed. She provided the garden spot, seed, and fertilizer. They both picked and sprayed for the bugs. Once when I asked her why she planted such a big garden she responded, "One seed is for bad weather. One seed is for the bugs. One seed is for Ol'Jim. And the last seed is for me."

The always-kept-locked cellar door was off of the kitchen in an adjacent hallway. I knew that it was kept locked not so much to keep the grandchildren out, as much as keeping whatever horrible things that lived in the dark and damp air in their hole. I imagined that if they saw the light, they would prowl around waiting to bite my flesh when I fell asleep at night. I always checked that door before I went to my room. The thought of going into that place scared me. "But Grandma, nobody likes beets." I prayed she would agree and forgive the order.

She looked at my mother, "Now he wants to tell me what to cook."

My mother stood up for her, "Jasper, do what you Grandmother says. Get the beets and don't argue."

I stood before my executioners. Surely death and destruction would follow me for all the days of my life. This was the end. I would never be a teenager. I felt the sweat on my palms. I rubbed them on my trousers. "But the door is locked," I meekly rebutted.

My mother let out an exasperating sigh, wiped her hand on a dish cloth, and pushed me out the kitchen into the hallway at the cellar door. She turned the key and pulled the door open. A blast of cool, moist air pushed against my face. I could smell the rot that bugs liked to hide beneath. I could smell the mold of things that had died and were in some stage of decomposition. I knew that there was evil in the darkness below. The gnawing hunger in my stomach was replaced with anxiety. I wished with all my heart that I had gone outside to play. I wished that I had stayed out all day, ignoring the excitement of the delicious kitchen, and returned only reluctantly after numerous summons that dinner was ready, on the table, and the blessing was about to be given. It was too late.

My mother pushed at my back. "Go!", she commanded. I dug my heels and braced my arms against the door threshold.

"There is no light down there." I begged.

"The light is in the middle of the room. Pull the string. If the beets are up high on the shelf, get a chair. Be careful not to break any of her jars." She walked back to the kitchen and resumed her discourse on the sunday school picnic.

I stood on the threshold of my doom for what seemed to be an eternity. Every time I thought that I had the courage to take the first step, my feet wouldn't move. My mother stepped around into the hallway. "What is taking you so long?"

"I'm, I'm trying to get my eyes adjusted to the dark. I'm almost ready. Just another second or so. Don't you have a flashlight or something I could use?"

"Don't be silly. The light string is at the bottom of the steps. Be careful. These steps are steep."

Not only were the steps steep but they were open. There was a flimsy two-by-four hand rail for balance; that was little comfort. What really was on my mind was having no protection from things that might be hiding behind the steps. There were two zig-zag planks angled from the door opening to the floor covered with tread planks. There was no backing to prevent something from reaching through the step and grabbing my ankle. I decided on a plan of action. I would go down the steps backwards, facing the door opening and only occasionally snatching a glance over my shoulder to see if I was near the bottom. I could watch for movement with each

23

step. When the thing did grab me, I would already be facing my escape route. Yeah, that would work.

I took my first backward step. Yeah, though I walk through the valley of the shadow. SHADOW!. I was facing the wrong way to look for shadows in the darkness below. I stopped. My knees were shaking. I turned sideways and took another step pivoting my head from one side to study the darkness below and to the other side to look for any movement through the steps.

"I will fear no Evil." I whispered, "I know you are there. Just say something. Make a noise." I waited and listened but only could hear the scuffle of feet and clanging noises of utensil against a bowl in the kitchen near by. My knees were really knocking together. I had only taken four steps. There were nine more to go. After two more steps I might be able to see through the dim light into the beet place. I thought, "I hate beets. I hate people who eat beets. I hate the blood red color of beets. After today, I never want to see a beet for the rest of my life. Maybe I can get the legislature to pass a law outlawing beets."

I wish that I had a rod or staff to defend myself with. How stupid of me not getting a broom from the kitchen before...It would have been comforting. I had made a spear at home wedging a sharp rock into a split end of a stave, then wrapping it with leather. I could really use it now. My mouth was getting dry and I noticed that my heart was beginning to pound. I decided to make a run for it. It would be surprised if I charged it rather than letting it charge me.

I raced down the steps making as much noise as I could thinking that it would retreat back into its hiding place in fright. I reached for the string to the light in the place where it should have been handing. My arm was flailing the air. I leaped up. I jumped up and grabbed hands full of air. Nothing! Nothing! Then the door at the top of the steps slammed shut and I was in total darkness, cut off and sealed in my tomb.

I was so panicked that I could not get the voice out to scream. I could hear myself scream, but nothing came out of my mouth. Suddenly I heard it. It made a sound. My heart jumped out of my chest and my head started to spin around and around. That was all I remember as all my energy left my body. I collapsed on to the nasty, dirty, foul smelling, damp, bug-infested, spidery floor.

Somehow my Grandma's Tom cat had pushed its way through the abandoned coal shoot and while I lay upon the floor, stretched out upon my chest, and licked my face with its raspy tongue. This brought me to consciousness with the extraordinary thought that I was being tasted by the creature that had been waiting for me in the basement. I imagined that its big teeth were about to chomp a big bit out of me. I never really saw the cat. In any event as I knocked it off my chest with all my might and bolted for the steps, the animal disappeared somewhere into the darkness. It let out a blood curdling cry of anguish which propelled me all the more to stumble up the steps two or three at a time.

When I arrived at the kitchen breathing heavily and so pale as to solicit the remarks from my mom as she looked me over from head to foot, "Look at you! How did you get so dirty? You are pale enough to have seen a ghost. What are you up to?"

Grandma looked at me and said, "Where are my beets?"

I managed to gulp a swallow of air and responded, "Can't you send my sister? I've got to go outside and play."

As I dashed out the screen door the two of them looked at each other and smiled. "It works every time," my grandmother quipped.

# WHY-WHY

The chipper advisor pranced into the president's office to render the morning domestic briefing. Various subjects were introduced and reviewed in an efficient machine-like manner from a check list attached to a clipboard. Almost as an apologetic postscript, the advisor informed the president that the Yerkes Primate Research Center at Emory University in Decatur, Georgia, had successfully created a human embryo clone.

The President, with palms up, curled his fingers inward as in a demanding gesture, retorted, "And? And?" The advisor's focus dropped to the floor in a submissive manner.

"Well, not only is the cloning project a hot political and ecclesiastical potato, but federal research grant and aid money was in place to support the human life through volunteer hostesses, mostly incarcerated lifers. Uh, African-Americans with a promise of early parole. Everything was supposed to have been aborted in late term in accordance with the American Bioethics Advisory Commission's mandate but there was a leak and the Right-to-Lifers are at picket stations demanding live birth. One last thing. You are about to become the father to six exact twins."

"Okay. Okay. First of all assemble a top security team. Find out how my DNA preservatives have been compromised by the leak. Get the names and locations of the Hostesses in this location and the other nine. Get a full dossier of the Emory Tank in the project."

Slicing the air with a finger, "Twenty-four hours to get facts. Top end, forty-eight hours and its a dead issue. Kill any trace to my preservatives. I want to know how just how public the communication lines are. What does the press know? What information do they have access to? I want to come out squeaky clean. We have an election in eighteen months. This won't be an issue. Forty-eight hours. Top priority."

Simultaneously a tight group of four Emory Tankers were

gulping coffee in one corner of the break room. By intention they had gone beyond the original parameters of the cloning project -specifically, injecting the nucleus, which includes the genes from one adult donor, into an egg, less the nucleus from another donor. They had ventured into the forbidden zone beyond somatic cell nuclear transfer and implantation. They had used the laboratory facilities to create the Why-Why in three additional Hostesses.

Biologically, women are distinguished from males by the lack of a Y Chromosome. They have identical sets of the X, while males have a combination of the X and Y chromosomes. The Emory Tank had created the impossible Y-Y combination. A combination forbidden by GOD and, worst of all, every feminist organization on the face of the globe.

"Buddy, let me tell you, that if we alienate the women...well that is a lot of votes". The President's face was crimson red.

The Emory group of genetic scientists had to cover their back sides and still maintain control of the projects. The clones would be public information in a matter of hours. The existence of the secret project had, at all costs, to be maintained and controlled. They began to set into motion the extra-ordinarily clever cover to hide their creations.

They knew that the only way to sustain their creation for further live study into maturation was to leak the cloning project discreetly to the press. The Tankers wanted to know if the creation could be carried through full term without spontaneously generating natural abortion. What side effects would be generated in the Hostess? After birth, what physical attributes would the Y-Y posses in size, body hair, intelligence, blood chemistry, strength, and organ and reproductive capacity. Everything was an unknown; and an opportunity to create the Y-Y might never be within their grasp, especially with the clone control group.

Before the project commenced, pardons had been signed, new identities, names, personal histories, social security numbers, jobs, and locations had been arranged so that any link between the Hostesses and clone would be lost. The three special Hostesses of the Y-Y embryo were not only given the same designation but were provided with an immense sum of money to be paid upon the surrender of their birth-child.

The creation of identical clones was a top secret project authorized by the president. His private agenda was to populate the nation with a genetically pure copy of himself. They would be the seed of a new aristocratic race in what he had engineered to be a change of presidential prerogatives from election every four years to simply be replacement by a clone. A new dynasty of leadership was to be born and perpetuated like the Kennedy clan - born to lead eternally. He had indirectly set the American Life League into motion through an anonymous tip of the nature of the project and its location.

As with the Clones, the Why-Whys were live birth deliveries at Emory University Hospital. Each was supervised by one of the four team members. The birth certificates listed no father. The mother's name was a pseudonym without trace. The mothers disappeared in a well orchestrated movement without trace. The children were placed with surrogate mothers in various locations. A team member visited frequently, taking whatever tests were appropriate at the time.

The Why-Why children appeared above normal in all aspects of early development including organ function, body systems, and intelligence. However, they had a blood type that was not like the A, B and O. At around thirteen, they hit a growth spurt and became enormous in size and strength. They prodigiously grew thick body hair over their entire body, including the around the eyes and forehead. They looked more like a great gorilla than human. They devoured large quantities of fruit, nuts, and red meat. By the age of twenty-two, they were eight feet tall and weighed in at three hundred pounds. There was as much obvious difference between them and the normal male as there is between a normal male and a female.

By computer educational stimulation each had passed the

capacity of the Doctoral level in medical and biological sciences. On a scale of zero to four, they were projected to be at ten. Like their size they had enormous intellect. Each learned to self-test themselves and to analyze the results by comparing the findings to the clone population samples. Like the mule, each was sterile. However, this did not mean that they did not have desires, urges, and emotions.

They were totally unaware of the environment outside of their living area. They had no concept of how food was generated. It just appeared on regular intervals for their consumption. They knew nothing of civil rights. They were unaware that they could demand release from being held without permission. For the time being they were docile, happy, and well-cared for in an artificial laboratory environment.

It was on the occasion of the visit by Amy Levin, a research assistant who happened to be ovulating at the time, that the near rape and escape of the subject known as Emory Clint occurred. Sandra had violated the regulations of not entering the living quarters without an assistant with a stun gun. Entering when she was emitting strongly scented pheromone was taboo because of the obvious exciting reaction it brought to the hyper-sensitive males. It was the Labor Day holiday weekend and there just wasn't any additional staff available to cover all the rules. The guard at the monitoring station was soundly asleep as Emory Clint tripped off all the security devices as he walked out of the building.

Panic spread through out the Decatur-Atlanta mega-metro areas of sightings of Big Foot. He was smart and elusive and quickly adapted to living off the available resources. Hiding in the day and moving only in the darkness, he was eventually able to wait out his life expectancy in seclusion deep from habitation.

31

# LAST FIRE

A widowed old man has been diagnosed with advanced stages of cancer and given a year or less to live, maybe longer with chemo-therapy. The old man, in his mid seventies, had been a successful investment broker. He is well off. His two daughters are grown, one married with small children and living far away; the other is in jail on a drug charge. He is all alone.

Declining chemo-therapy, the old man buys a 150 acre farm in a remote holler in the mountains of North Carolina. He requests the owners not to move but to pay back a portion of the sale price monthly as rent. He builds a very modest house some distance from the tenants as his seclusion domicile residence. He wished to die in the woods at a camp fire.

The happiest times of his life were when he was a carefree youth camping with his buddies, singing songs, doing skits, roasting marshmallows and hot dogs, and telling scary stories. The balance of his life had been spent at the office earning the money that his wife and daughters lavishly spent. No matter how much he gave, it was never enough to satisfy them. They treated him with the utmost disrespect because he wouldn't give them everything. Because of this, they withheld their love and affection. He was used to being alone. He asked for nothing from them; they obliged.

A twelve-year-old kid is his neighborhood was the paper boy, who up until his wife's death and his own dismal health report, was only an occasional "Good morning" or an evening knock at the door for payment. The old man decided to befriend the boy. He asked the boy where he lived and visited with the mother who was a middle school cafeteria worker. The boy was an only child of a single mom. They both pretty much lived off money left by her father and which was held in trust. It is not enough. The grandfather had been a Sears & Roebuck store manager during affluent times and took all his bonuses in company stock.

The old man explained to her that he was lonely and

desired the companionship of the boy in going hunting, fishing, washing the car, and just simply having him check in on him regularly. He did not tell her or the boy that he was terminally ill or about the farm far away. At first she was very pleased that somebody wanted to pay attention to her child; but as the months pass, she became resentful that she had to share the boy with the old man. She could not compete with the gifts that the old man gave to the boy, which the boy called "Treasure". He saw the kid partly as himself at that age and partly as the son that he wished that he had. The mother complained to the old man that the very reason that she had a child was to have something that would love her.

The old man persuaded the mother by setting up a generous trust for the boy's education plus handsome monthly annuities to both of them for the duration of their lives. He also provided lump sum disbursements in the event should a crisis arise requiring extraordinary money. Unknown to the child, the mother was very happy with the financial arrangement although she suspected that the old man was a pervert. He told her that she could quit her job at the school, buy new clothes, and get social with men. She could start her life all over again. The old man gave her the deed to his house.

The old man had the mother sign a document just short of the legal requirements for adoption that allowed the old man to have full custody of the boy until he was twenty-one. In essence the mother had sold her child. The papers were signed on her birthday and coincidental with the beginning of summer vacation. A few days later the old man and boy vanished to the farm.

The old man purchased a go-cart, horse, and lots of fire works to amuse the boy during the first week. During the second week they Ki-yacked the French Broad River and hiked a portion of the Appalachian Trail East of Roan Mountain. They went to the Charlotte Panthers Game and to Carrowinds and to the Winston Cup stock car race in North Wilkesboro. On every trip, the boy would search the crowds for a familiar face. He would separate himself from the old man and get lost in a pretend kind of way. He scared the old man frequently by being found talking to strangers and hanging out outside of the men's room. They spent more time at the farm taking long walks in the woods, fishing, and playing in the streams. They dug crayfish and planned to build bridges that the old man would never see.

He confided in the boy about his death wish to expire at a campfire. He made the boy promise that if anything happened, he would get him to the campfire. He taught the boy how to build a fire and they cooked hot dogs and roasted marshmallows often. They told each other stories and jokes. The laughed and laughed in great thundering volleys. The old man forgot his pain and destination. He became slower, weaker, and needed more rest. It became more difficult for the old man to climb the hill to the fire ring. They stopped going. Instead they played cards, checkers, and chess at the house.

In the house, there was no telephone, television, or radio. The tenants, who were both on their second failing married were admonished to lock their house when they were absent. The boy was prohibited by the old man from entering the tenants' house with out his presence and permission on the grounds that they smoked pot. They had a large window at ground level through which the TV could be seen. When the old man slept, the boy would slip into the night to sit in the yard to play with the dogs and cats and to watch TV unknown to the tenants. Occasionally he would cry for his mother in whose lap he would lie at home while watching TV on the couch. Eventually he was discovered by the tenants.

The boy told the tenants how much he missed his mother and wanted to talk to her. He really wanted to go home. After all, the food that the old man ate was not what he liked. (The old man lived on fruit and vegetables). The boy said that he had never lived in a house with a man whose snoring was so annoying. He told them that the old man was not a relative but had not hurt or mistreated him in any way. He said that he was bored. He hated picking up after himself and having to take his turn at cleaning. His mom never made him do anything like put his toys and games away. He always got his way. He never had to share. He hated to have someone tell him to brush his teeth or to take a bath or to pick up the towel and his dirty clothes.

The old man was getting slower and weaker as his cancer spread throughout his body. The pain pills only made him more lethargic. He fell asleep before the boy when reading the bedtime classics to him. He was leaving the house less often. The boy thought that something might be wrong but never asked. The tenant woman stopped by the house one morning on her way to work as a waitress at a local eatery to tell the old man about the boy sitting outside of their window at night. She also told him that the boy was not happy and wanted his mother. The tenant lady talked about the boy and old man with the cook at work. The cook suggested that maybe the boy had been abducted during a parental custody dispute. She told the cook that they boy was not related to the old man. They both decided that the boy had been kidnapped and called Tom at the County Sheriff's Department.

Tom and three fellow officers in two cruisers introduced themselves to the old man within the hour and explained the reason for the visit. The old man produced the documents showing that he had legal custody of the child. The boy was taken into protective custody until the mother and district attorney could be reached to verify the documents. The mother now knew the location of her son. The old man and boy were returned to the farm.

The boy laid asleep in his bed as the old man lay awake suffering his last few moments of life, not being at the campfire. The old man struggled to evacuate his reading chair only to collapse on the floor. He pulled himself to the bedside of the boy whose hand was hanging by the bedside outside of the covers. The old man reached up and touched it, he held it gently in his own hand. The old man could feel the boy's warmth and the pulsing of the boy's heart. He lifted the hand and gently pressed it to his cheek knowing that this would be his last mortal act on earth. The boy woke and asked, "What are you doing". The old man replied that he just wanted to say good-bye. The boy closed his eyes and returned to sleep. The old man crumbled on the floor and expired.

The mother arrived early the next morning with Tom from the Sheriff's Department to wake the child. They banged at the door. The boy stumbled on the cold and open-eyed old man on the floor by the side of his bed. He knew instinctively that the old man was dead. The boy and mother embraced. The boy broke his embrace with his mother, and while brushing the tears from his eyes declared that the old man was dead. He ran back inside the house and fell on the old man with as much affection as he had given his mother just moments before. The boy became possessed to fulfil the old man's death wish. With the help of Tom and his mother, they carried the old man up the hill to the fire ring where the boy built a fire and sang solo for the last time the old man's favorite song.

TRETTER 97

# BED BUGS DON'T BITE

The day that Barry's father was placed in the grave, his dad's office burned. No, it was not arson. The fire started from a short in the insulation of a power transformer under the building, then spread up and into an interior wall. The firemen were on the spot within thirty minutes after receiving a report from a kid on a bike who saw smoke. The fire station, two doors away, extinguished the smoldering floor seals by turning off the building power. The office was shouldered on one side by a concrete wall twenty feet high and on the other two sides by a parking lot. A fire could not have spread to adjoining property. Their energy must have been at an all time peak as they kicked down the doors, knocked out the windows and flooded the interior with a deluge of water. The medical equipment was ruined, the patient files and X-Rays were soaked. The $100,000 X-Ray machine was hacked to death in an attempt to access the interior wall. The floors buckled from the water saturation and subsequent swelling. The plastered walls cracked from the un-vented heat. The building was in ruins not so much form the small contained fire but, by far, more from the attempt to discover and to extinguish the source of smoke.

There is a law on the books that a claimant must receive a settlement offer in a reasonable period of time. Unfortunately, our great protectors neglected to define the amount of reasonable time or to put any bite into the law with fines or a license revocation for infractions. After a month, a dozen phone calls, a dozen visits to Hickory, a dozen letters to various insurance representatives, then finally, a check for $20,000 was received as a settlement on a $200,000 loss. By the time the check was received, the building had been thoroughly vandalized and had to be bulldozed and hauled away. A lifetime of memories were gone. His father had placed the property in his name as security against a nuisance malpractice lawsuit. He always boasted that in fifty-three years of medical practice, he had never been sued.

Barry left town and deposited the money in the North Wilkesboro Savings and Loan, near his father's old home-place.

He had no idea how long he would remain at the country home-place or how long the money would last. He had no plan except that he had a lot of thinking to do on his own, away from the confusion and sympathy of well intending friends. The old house on the place had been rented to a caretaker who made repairs as necessary and mowed the grass around the scattered buildings. He and his wife had other regular town-jobs. They welcomed him as the new landlord of the property. Barry asked for and was granted permission to use the bathroom and kitchen during his stay. They were very congenial people.

Immediate shelter was found in an old, neglected grain barn which was sixteen feet wide and twenty-four feet long. The building was dilapidated but appeared to be structurally sound. It was capped with a rusty galvanized tin roof. A path had to be hacked through the tall grass, honeysuckle vines, and blackberry bushes to access the opening above the rotted steps. The building was nearly completely overgrown and covered with vines and hidden by privet bushes of enormous size and density. Only one corner was visible to give an indications that a building was somehow buried in the thicket. It was more reclaimed by nature than useful to human inhabitants. Inside were the accumulation of twenty years of tenant discards packed into the abandoned building. After he had removed about forty bundles of pink fiberglass insulation, there was enough room to open the hand-made plank door to allow light to penetrate. He sized up the situation. Two additional days would be required to empty the building, to haul off non-salvageable junk, and to burn the trash. In his Honda wagon were a table, chair, typewriter, camping stove, utensils, tools, and a footlocker with an assortment of clothes. He borrowed some tools and got to work.

Before his abrupt departure, he had taken time to notified the church secretary that she would have to fill his post during his absence. The folks at work knew what he was going through and were probably glad to see him leave. Although they had sympathy, they were disassociated with his intense grief. He and his wife, Jane, parted with a warning from her, "Now don't go up there and mull over this thing." His newly widowed mother was told that he had gone to visit the farm on business. Finally after repeated calls, Jane told her that he was troubled over the death of his father and would be home shortly. The folks at the church sensed that something was wrong when Jane appeared at their customary pew without him. The tongues whispered that Barry and Jane were probably separated or about to be divorced. The gossipers didn't have the courage to ask directly.

He left Jane instructions on how to file the state sales tax returns for South Carolina; how to file the withholding tax returns for both the federal government and for the state; how to fill in the unemployment tax forms for both states and the federal government; how to file the federal and state corporate income tax forms; how to file the city and county property taxes, how to file the intangible taxes; and lastly how to compute the workman's compensation insurance fees to keep their small business going without interruption. He had to take precautions because he didn't know how long he would be on sabbatical.

Occasionally he wrote letters or made an evening phone call when he knew that Jane had finally settled from her busy schedule. She was so very kind not burdening him with mechanical repertory of business or family problems. He didn't want to hear any more bad news. He needed to repair himself, to put himself back together, and to heal from the pain. He had to do it by himself. It would take time for the scar to form in his heart over the open wound of heart break. For the time being his pain was intolerable, and on more than one occasion while in route to the rural place, contemplated veering off the highway at high speed and into a phone pole. He couldn't do this to his wife and children.

"How are the kids?"

"The kids are busy and the business could always use your touch. But how are you doing?" She retorted.

"I'm feeling better. I'm not so edgy. I get up at first light and go to the main house to fix coffee and to make breakfast. I work all day until twilight, take a shower and fix supper. I've lost some weight and have tightened up a lot of flab. I'm getting addicted to this peace and quiet and sweet well water. I think that I might be ready for a good woman or a fight which ever gets here first."

By the next weekend the whole kitten caboodle arrived. Their arrival was the first break that he had seen in a month since arriving at the farm. After exchanging hugs and kisses, she put the kids to bed in the rear of the van then crawled into the make-shift bed with him. Her presence was the only touch that he had with reality. She was warm, soft, and had a reassuring familiarity. The next morning a trip to Stone Mountain to hike and picnic with the family was organized. When she and the children left, it was as though his reason for living had just been reaffirmed.

The barn had been constructed to cure and store agricultural products to be fed to stock during the winter months. As he dug into the piles of discard, he uncovered letters that Jane and he had exchanged prior to their marriage. The reading of these letters gave him amusement and courage to look beyond the immediate past. The letters took him back to a time when he was full of vinegar and spit in stark contrast to his present depressed disposition. He was free and full of dreams of what life would promise for the two of them. The mice had gnawed at the glue on the envelopes, the elements had aged the stationary but the sensation of excitement burst from the yellowed pages. Without the visit, without the letters, without the fond memories cuddled in a secure place, he would have died of grief. Jane put things succinctly for all times. She loved him. She had given her life to him as he had given his to her. He read the letters and the Bible nightly before retiring.

When Jane and the children visited, the barn was in the midst of transformation. He had decided to use the insurance money to convert the grain barn into a habitable vacation cottage. The project kept him busy. His mind was off of his despair and grief. It put time between him and the death of his father. Oh, how he had worshiped the old man. They had grown to be best friends. They shared every inner-most thought. They had bonded into one person with two personalities. This project filled his thoughts and time completely. It was so therapeutic; he was rebuilding his life nail by nail.

The task to reconstruct the granary into a domicile was staggering. As he crawled under the foundation and placed stones and wedges, it was his life and the floor which was being leveled. As he pushed walls back into a vertical position, it was his life that found a plumb center. As gravel was poured onto the weathered drive, it was his life that received the new foundation. It was not a vacation home that he was building, but a new life. He ate balanced simple meals, exercised from dawn to dusk, slept soundly, and flushed his system with the artesian well water. He was building courage and endurance. Daily, his insecurity and despair was undergoing a metamorphosis. He was gaining control. He were prevailing. Barry needed new structure in his life. With each hammer blow, each board cut, with each measurement taken, Barry repaired himself. The building was still far from being hospitable; and Barry, likewise, was not finished with himself.

Years before when the a local lumber company went out of business, he had bought building materials at below cost. He would now use them in the project. He had windows, the fireplace mantel, tiles and three sets of bunk beds stored in the building. The cabinets came from his Charleston home garage; the refrigerator was a cast-off from his mother's kitchen in Hickory.

While he and Jane attended First Presbyterian Church near the farm when they were first married, the ladies of the church decided that the cemetery behind the church should be surrounded by a chain link fence instead of the loose rock wall. The Elders had allocated money for a fence but searched for a means to have the old wall removed at no cost. They had agreed that the honeysuckle vines and the snake, seen several years prior, were sufficient reasons for a change. The church cemetery wall had been a fixture of the church for in excess of two hundred years. It had been constructed by members of generations past who conveyed rock in lieu of spiritual donation in coin. Barry bought the rock from the stone fencing for the sum of eighty dollars and had it delivered to the home place not really knowing what he would ever do with the stone. The sabbatical gave him the perfect opportunity to arrange the stone into a wall which would support a porch to be extended from the front of the grain barn. There were some stones in the pile that, if lifted, would have ruptured his heart. There were also some stones that displayed vague lettering as though they may have been grave markers.

The two narrow sides of the building were vertically slatted with two inch boards spaced so as to allow air to freely ventilate and to cure the grain and the tobacco. He tore out the slatting and braced the openings with two-by-fours in fear that the entire building might collapse upon him. The thought crossed his mind more than once that the building might come down during his labors or slumber. What a tragic end. What a cheat it would be to the devil for him to have a quick and easy demise.

At first the days and nights were hot and he slept under a single sheet to keep the bugs off; but as the weeks passed, the sheet and double folded army blanket were inadequate. He began to sleep with socks and a jogging suit and still shivered during waking moments. In the early morning as the sun stirred him from his nest, he noticed that his humid breath had frozen on the blanket during the night and would sparkle like jewels. Its illusion would only last for a minute until the light beams evaporated the glistening gems.

One memorable night was when there was a new moon, the weather turned nasty. Storm clouds often appeared late in the afternoon but usually they would pass to drop bolts of lightning elsewhere. That would not be the case, they would pass directly over his humble abode on this evening. He could hear the rolling thunder like mortar percussions rocking the earth in some distant battle for dominion over civil rights. The noise woke him. Unknown to him, the National Weather Service has issued a Severe Weather Advisory Bulletin for the county. Hurricane force winds could be expected. A Tornado Watch was in effect. It was nature's way of letting mortals know that we do not have dominion over the Earth. He began to count the seconds from streak to sound and to calculated the storm to be five miles distant. Sleep would be impossible. The seconds-count were of increasingly shorter durations, the storm was a few miles away and closing in on his direction. For some insane reason, he felt more secure with his eyes open even though he couldn't see a thing in the pitch black.

The wind began to blow hardily. The leaves rattled in the mighty persimmon and pear trees in a protest to the storm. They were frightened that they might be hurt. The lightning struck again and again giving flickering sight in the night like the effect of a strobe light. The thunder came again and again almost without interruption. The vibrations felt like mini earthquakes. It was a violent war between the earth and the sky. As if the light and sounds were not enough, the sky broke into torrents of fist-size rain drops beating the leaves into silence and submission. With the equal suddenness of the rain, the lightening ceased as though someone was flipping switches off and on.

The wind swept the violence through the open cabin, across his bed, and onto his face. His senses were saturated with the sensations of lightning and thunder. He could feel the tears from Heaven's rage on his face. Suddenly, he was aware that he was not alone in the open room. There was no door; there were two open walls; anything could enter without obstruction. He could smell the unmistakable stench of moisture on a furry creature's coat. Whatever it was, it was close, very close. An animal's sense of smell and night-sight are 10,000 more acute when compared to those of a simpler God-fearing human's. Compared to the unknown intruder's senses, Barry's were dulled from ages of neglect of forest survival. If this would be the end, if this would be the night visitor he had experienced a decade-and-half ago, then so let it be. He would not succumb this time without facing it eye-to-eye.

Barry knew there was a ghost at the farm. It was his own personal ghost because nobody else had confessed to having had an experience with it. Barry was almost embarrassed to mention it because people thought him to be a fool. Barry had to live comfortably knowing that it was real. He had seen it or rather felt its presence and touch. It spoke to him. It took almost all of his first twenty years of life to overcome his fear of being alone in the dark and of being afraid of being destroyed by lightening. His soul was being tested by the Power of God tonight. Everything that was happening was not just coincidental. He was having to face again all his childhood fears one by one.

The ghost, which he called David, had been his first exposure to the Super Natural. The encounter occurred on a night so dark that he could not see his hand in front of his face. He had to trust that all his other senses told him that his hand was indeed in front of his face. The sound of something pushing on the exterior of the clap-board sided home-place woke him. The add-on room of the old shot-gun house was at ground level with three sides exposed. He could hear the boards creak and crack from something pushing against it with a lot of force. It was not a pounding or knocking sound. It moved from one exposure side to the next like it would work it's way around the house. It pushed again but the building resisted. An eighteen-light window almost from floor to ceiling high was between the thing and the next corner. He imagined the next forceful push would cause the window to burst into the room. Barry's scalp was tingling with goose-bumps. His mouth was dry. His heart was pounding with anxiety. He knew it wasn't anybody, at this late hour, trying to play a prank on him.

Like his hand in front of his face, all his senses told him something was out there. Of this, he was certain. Something

46

out there was trying to find an opening to get inside. With this thought, he was afraid to be certain. Barry knew that it had to be an enormous creature with more weight and brawn than a human to make the siding crack. He thought maybe it was a rogue black bear; maybe not. But wouldn't a bear grunt or groan like we do when it exerted a tremendous effort, he asked himself? But then, he thought, bears don't push with a steady force; they rock trees with pulsating motion. His chain of thoughts were interrupted by a forth sound of moaning boards and squeaky rusted nails. It was now past the window but still on the same side; Barry kept absolutely motionless. The last side of the house had a porch attached to it. The intruder would have to go around the pillars and railings to find the next window or door. Barry waited for what seemed like an eternity, but was in reality only a few minutes, waiting for the continuation of noises. There would be no more and Barry finally fell back to sleep convinced that the sounds were just noises of an old house settling on its foundation.

Barry was mistaken. He was wrong. It was not over; it was just the beginning of the most, scary night of his life.

The second time Barry woke from a comfortable sleep that night was when he sensed, like his hand, that something was in the room with him. The sensation was immediate. His awakening was a sudden snap like the reaction one has to a loud alarm clock ring. Barry knew it was in the room. He couldn't see it; he couldn't hear it; he couldn't smell it; and he didn't want to search for it. There was no way he was going to get out of bed and cross the room to flip the overhead light switch by the side of the door. Barry was not that brave. In fact at this moment he was cowering with his covers pulled up nearly over his face. His knees were pulled to his chest. His elbows were tucked close to his sides. He sat in total darkened silence waiting for what would happen next. Until now Barry did not believe that a person could die from fright. He really only thought to be "scared to death" was only a trite phrase. He knew better now. His heart could not take much more before it exploded. All his thoughts accumulated to a fleeting few seconds.

Then the most terrible sound occurred in the far corner of the room to confirm what he knew was true. There was something in the room with him. It wasn't a loud sound at all. It was the sound a floor board makes when the weight of a foot is either placed on it or removed from it. In any event, the things was there and moving. Barry knew he had to scream or go crazy, but he was shaking so violently with fear he couldn't get his throat unfrozen to make a sound. When the board squeaked one step closer to him, he did scream. He realized that his scream sounded more like a yell for mercy from God than at the thing that was slowly moving toward him. Tears flooded down his cheeks and dripped off his chin. In a hysterical, cracking, high-pitched voice, he begged the thing not to hurt him. He used words like "God" and "Please" sincerely for the first time in his narcissistic life.

Without hearing a sound, a calming voice came into Barry's mind. "I've come to get you." It put a reassuring hand on his shoulder. It was a kind and gently touch. Barry received it that way. His fright had completely vanished. The soothing male voice continued, "Are you ready to go?"

Barry knew instinctively that if he answered in the affirmation, his life was over and his soul would be transported to the hereafter by the intruder. Totally calmed, Barry answered, "No. I haven't got started yet". Barry knew that his whole life up to this point had been selfish. He had done nothing to make the world a better place. He hadn't done anything for anybody out of the kindness of his heart. His whole life added up to a big zero. To this point, Barry knew that whether he lived, died, or never existed at all, made no difference. Barry understood his life was about to change.

The next morning Barry searched the ground outside of his room for the bear prints. There weren't any.

Back in the grain barn, Barry's BIC lighter was on the footlocker, next to a candle stub. He had no flashlight. He wished and prayed with all his heart that whatever was in the cabin with him would go away. He momentarily imagined that he was hallucinating, in a dream, or not in the place where he was. This was not happening. This demon-devil creature of the night was not going to get him. Please God don't let it get me. His heart was raceing into his throat and pounding at his brain. He took a deep breath and held it so that he could quiet his body rhythm. He listened. There was no sound.

He slowly eased his hand from under the covers in the direction of the lighter pretending that his hand would not draw the attention of the intruder. He held it momentarily to see; it would tempt the creature. Nothing happened. He pushed his forearm slowly from under the covers, The light bed covering gave him a false sense of security. Only inches existed between his fingers and a light to illuminate the unknown intruder. Suddenly he froze. He could hear movement through the drumming of rain on the tin roof. Then something bumped the bed. "Jesus!"' he wanted to scream. The thing was next to him. His heart pounded with surges of adrenaline. Then something touched his arm. He could feel the hair on his head stand at attention. The sensation on his arm was not a bite It was not a lunge at his throat like he was envisioning the end of his life to be; it was just a gentile touch. His arm jutted the distance and grabbed the lighter.

When the room was illuminated, he could only see a large bundle of fur. His eyes had not adjusted to the light well enough to determine immediately what kind of creature stood before him. He would have sacrificed an arm or hand if necessary but he would not have gone down for the full count easily. Whatever it was had short hair and was about dog size. His focus was rapidly improving. A German shepherd just like the one that had killed his two hundred and fifty pound steer was poised at his bed, ears perked, mouth open. His big, red, moist tongue dangled - a possible sign of a lack of interest in having his pounding heart for diner.

"Sit!" He commanded. The animal's head swayed from side to side; its ears dropped as it fell to the floor in compliance. Thank God, he thought.

The storm was now overhead. The sight and sound were almost simultaneous. The dog quivered. "Good Boy," he said with a soothing voice. His heart began to find normal rhythm. Barry lit the candle and lifted it from the locker and placed it on the bed corner as he swung his feet to the floor. He leaned forward and opened the locker and extracted his poncho which he spread on top of the covers to barrier himself from the wisps of rain. The dog put its head between its paws on the floor. Barry knew that the animal wouldn't be a problem. His stench overwhelmed the ozone in the air, but at least the dog momentarily had company in Barry's presence. The candle flickered and extinguished from the breath of the violent storm. He grabbed the lighter and set the flame again.

The roof of the barn was covered in tin - an attraction ten-to-one over the pear and persimmon trees which soared to the heavens in grateful admiration to the sun's warmth and light. Would his destruction be usurped to an inert tin-skin cabin shared by a man and a dog both of which were seeking shelter from the cruel and inhospitable world? The storm was at full force.

The flashes and sound seemed more separate. He counted the seconds- two, then three, and more and more. It was beyond us now. There was light and pounding as before, but its direction was certain to be moving away. The wick was sniffed and he nestled back into the covers. When he woke the dog was gone. It had familiarized itself to him during the night, but had struck out on its own possibly to join a pack before daybreak. He would have to track and kill the animal before the sun set.

Barry dressed for the deep woods and went to the main house for coffee and breakfast. He returned to the cabin and opened the footlocker. He had brought a Colt 22 semiautomatic target pistol with a ten cartridge clip. He popped the clip into the gun grip and headed back to the main house where the trail began to the bottom and creek. The dog would certainly head in this direction for a morning drink. He stepped across the rocks and spotted some tracks leading into a ravine. He pulled back the action of the pistol placing a shell in the chamber and pushed on the safety catch. The ground was wet from the night's rain, so leaves and twigs would not crunch or rustle under foot. He moved very cautiously. The air was dead calm; his scent would not carry quickly. These were two distinct advantages that he had to play in his favor.

He moved about ten feet into the ravine. It narrowed to a width of about ten feet and a good flow of runoff was in the bed. He looked up and saw a catamount sleeping on a fallen tree that stretched across the banks of the ravine. The cat was at head height and about twenty feet away. The cat had not sensed his presence but lay with all four paws dangling. Would it spring and run or lunge in panic at him? The dog and cat were natural enemies. How could it be so relaxed with the large shepherd nearby? He had to have mistaken the tracks. He looked to the left for a root or bolder to drop behind - nothing. When he looked to the right, he saw a copperhead coiled in position to strike. He was only several feet away from his face. He didn't bat an eye. He thought, "Yea, tho I walk through the valley of the shadow of death, I shall fear no evil..." The snake whipped its tongue several times and stared with beady eyes. He could have shot at the catamount or the snake but not both. One would get me, one would die. The snake uncoiled and slithered into a hole in the bank of the ravine. Barry guessed that he was no threat or that he was too large to be swallowed for breakfast.

Barry began to back up. The catamount never stirred. The cat was as rare in these parts as an eagle. It was at the top of the food chain. The range of the animal was considered to be in terms of thousands of acres; Barry would do everything to make it feel at home. He had a dual reason for wanting the dog exterminated. Such a dog would run this cat up a tree then call the pack to stand patrol until the animal either stood to fight or died of thirst. Such a vigil could last for several days. If the cat didn't come down promptly, its chances to run in a weakened state and survive were greatly diminished. On the other hand, dogs were not only common, but a hazard to life and stock. Metropolitan inhabitants would buy a cute little puppy; but when they began to reach an unruly adult temperament, the owner would set them free into the country. For the shepherds of cattle, these shepherds of Germany were a liability. They would join into packs, stalk and kill farmer's stock for survival. A few could be domesticated into the roll of house security, but the hundreds turned into the country on a yearly basis greatly outpaced the absorption of the animal into domestic service. The balance of the animals became diseased, destroyed small game, natural habitat, stock and generally upset the natural order of the succession in the forest. He had no second thoughts concerning keeping the order intact. In fact, he considered the killing of stray dogs as a neighborly duty. The dog that he hunted was a silver haired shepherd; well worth $500.00 from a pet store or breeder if pedigreed. A prize yearling bull could be worth several thousand.

He went back to the main house for a second cup of coffee, thus giving the cat time to finish the nap and to move on. The shepherd languished up to him at the house. His tail wagged as Barry pulled the pistol from beneath his belt. He called, "Here," and slapped his thigh thus mimicking obedience school techniques of control. He lowered his left hand and leaned down as though Barry were about to feed the animal table scraps. He then leveled the pistol between the eyes and fired. The dog stopped and fell. He fired another shot between the ears. It rolled onto a side. The shepherd's legs quivered in resistance for a few seconds as it's life abruptly ended.

Barry suddenly felt a tremendous fright overtake him. Somehow the destruction of the stray dog had become one and the same as his emotion with his father's death. Had he imagined that his father had been in his pistol sights? His hands began to shake and his legs became unsteady as visions of the recent funeral snapped by. He had to sit down and compose himself. Barry dug a hole under a low gum tree branch at the corner of the pasture farthermost from the main house. He gently placed the dog in the shallow grave and recited a few words that he really meant for his father. Alone now, tears streamed down his cheeks as he finally released the power of his full emotions. Feelings that he had not until now been able to release. With each shovel of dirt sprinkled on the dog's carcass, he let go of his father.

He called Jane for news. She said. "Its time for you to come home."

He understood and headed for his cabin. Time had been illusive. He was not quite sure if he had been gone for ten weeks or two months. P hysically, he felt changed, strong, and had wind in his sails. He would miss the fresh artesian well-water and a morning cup of coffee. He had enamored himself in pure country dialogue about just how big Dolly Parton's breasts really were; whose football team would rain supreme; and which local restaurant made the best cup of coffee and chile. Most importantly, he had lain his father to rest with an inner peace. He realized that his pain was the natural healing process and that the continued remembrances of love were the therapeutic salve. What a relief he felt to hear the simple uncomplicated response when he told Jane that he would be home in a few days to enjoy his birthday.

54

# FOURTH LEVEL

"Did you leave your wedge at the third hole?"

Searching his bag, "Well, yes I must have."

"Don't worry. The groundskeeper has it on his cart. Wave him down."

After Jack got the attention of the passing cart driver and retrieved his club, he returned to where Randy was waiting. "How did you know that he had it? Are you clairvoyant of something?"

"Its just something that I do. I'm sorry. I didn't mean to ...I try not to be .... You can do me a big favor and not say anything about this."

While Randy was teeing-up for his drive at the ninth hole, Jack asked, "Did you really read his mind? Can you read my mind or, better yet, my wife's? If you can do that, then you might be the most important man on the face of the Earth!"

"No. It's not what you think. Not at all." Randy knew that everybody always tried to find closure for things about which they have no understanding, no perception, and no cognitive penetration. "The mind is a tool capable of more than deductive, copying, or inductive reasoning."

"What do you mean?" Jack teed-up after Randy took his drive.

"The easiest thought process is to make a deductive conclusion such as: one plus one equals two. The next more complex thought pattern is when you copy one set of deductions and apply them to a new parameter. Let me give you an example. If you follow a recipe to make peanut butter cookies; then, with a little insight, you can make oatmeal cookies. A more complex thought process is required to come up with an array of inductive incidents that will produce the answer of "Two" or "Cookie". You expand your field of inquiry by broadening its level to the infinite power. The process is also quite an extraordinarily stimulating mental process."

Jack laughed. "I could not imagine reading a book about the number 'Two'. That would be the ultimate bore."
Randy quipped. "Yes, it would. But let me remind you that our wives buy cookbooks all the time. It is not beyond the stretch of logic to have one published on the subject of 'Cookies'. Grant me that."
"Well, okay." They were both putting out. Randy was tending the flag. "I just can't get over this. It must be a wonderful gift."
"No, it's not. It is just the opposite. I try to block it out. Turn if off."
"Why?"
"It's a nuisance. It's a distraction and I cause confusion."
"How?"
"I can walk down a street and pass person after person, all of whom have pain that they are dealing with. They are silently screaming for help. Part of the reason that I enjoy playing golf with you is because you don't have pain. Your life is normal and you are a happy person."
"Thank you. I appreciate your compliment."
"I can also beat you. You play a lousy game of golf."
"I'm trying to improve. You have got to give me that."
Randy looked at Jack and lifted his eyebrows as though he was questioning the truth of Jack's statement. "Well, maybe a little bit. Hey, cut it out. You're screwing with my mind. Aren't you?"
"When have you ever had a birdie on a hole?"
"I've had nice drives. I have had a few nice chips and some great putts. It's just that my game hasn't come together all in one hole."
"Is that why you try to block it out?" Jack answered his own question, "Because there is so much torment and suffering?"
"It gets to you after a while. You want to get away from it. Far away, deep in a hole underground to insulate yourself from the stacks and piles of grief. It turns you bitter."
"Were you born with it? Is it natural?" Jack asked after

a long pause.

"No not really. I guess that there is some genetics or a maturation process involved, but mostly it is the fourth level of cognitive ability - beyond the Cookie."

Jack chewed and swallowed the sentence in silence. "Okay, I'll fall for it. And what is the fourth level, or is there a need for me to ask?"

"This one is not easy to explain. At some time in your life you have experienced a situation where you and somebody else have a simultaneous thought. I don't mean when you are eating dinner with your wife and pass her the salt because you know that, without asking, she will want the salt shaker. This behavior is acquired learning. You have been taught to expect to pass the salt from repetition of having to do it so often. It is a different process when you are able to think consecutively with a stranger. It takes immense concentration to pass a thought. It takes equally acute perception to be able to discern a thought that belongs to another. This is a preternatural process that is strange and inexplicable."

Randy continued as he pulled his putter from his golf bag, "When a person is in psychological pain, all they can think of is finding a solution. They radiate a cerebral broadcast. They beg for help. They are totally consumed in their thoughts to the exclusion of anything else. They are blinded by it. I have a sensitive antenna. I pick up their broadcasts. If you stopped a person on the street and asked what was wrong, then you better find a bench because they will pour it out. They seek solutions, redemption, forgiveness, and most importantly they want to transfer their pain to somebody else. Anybody will do, even a stranger."

"Can you do it with me?"

"I don't know. What frequency do you broadcast on?" Randy poped open Jack's comfortable closure.

"I don't know. I'm new at this. How do I begin."

"Don't. It's dangerous." Randy stated with a firm voice. They were finishing at the twelfth hole.

"How so?"

"I've covered this ground. Once you find your frequency, are able to get confirmation, able to broadcast,... well, then you thirst for the ability to receive the thoughts and messages. He picked up his bag and began to walk to the golf cart. With fingers fanned, aimed, and shaking like loaded pistols, Randy turned to Jack. He begged, "Let's not do this conversation, okay?"

"No. Back up. Calm down. I mean, come here." Jack placed a hand on Randy's shoulder as a confirmation of confidence. "I want to talk about this antenna, cognitive broadcast, level four business, whatever. I want to understand it, not do it. Okay? I mean are you for real or are you just packing my head with a bunch of BS. I really mean that this is about the wildest thing I have ever heard in my life."

Randy said, "Why don't we talk about something else. All this is really making me nervous. I don't want to be rear-ended with ridicule."

"I promise that I won't repeat this conversation with a living soul. This is as confidential as a tax return."

"Tax return?"

"Okay. Confession to a priest. Tax return was a bad choice."

"No. Neither. I'm really tired. Do you want to play this out by yourself? Give me a four over par on the next three holes and I still beat you."

As Randy began his walk back to the clubhouse Jack retorted, "You're afraid or you're a hoax. One or the other."

"I already knew that you would say that. It doesn't matter if you mean my golf score or your lost clubs. It's all the same, Jack - the living or the non-living." Randy waived a hand and called, "Later."

Jack put his clubs into the cart, "Jesus, now what have I done?" He pulled up along side of Randy. "I'm sorry about calling you a hoax. Jump in and I'll buy you a beer in the Clubhouse. On the way they sat silently until Jack broke the ice, "I'm thinking of a number between zero and five hundred."

"I don't do numbers."

"What do you mean you don't do numbers. That is a cop-out answer. I give you one good chance to convince me you are for real and your refuse to play the game you started."

"I don't do numbers. I just don't do numbers. If I did, you would haul me to the nearest LOTTO dealer to buy tickets. I don't do numbers."

"Why?"

"It would interrupt the natural course of events. If you want to win or lose, you play the odds on your own. Numbers and machines don't transmit or receive thoughts. They have no psycho phenomena."

"What color am I thinking of?"

"Black. And black is not a color; it is the total absence of color. Nice try, but I don't think you're ready."

"I admit that I am ignorant about this psycho stuff because it's all new to me. I've got no experience with it or at least I don't think that I have. How would I know if I was experiencing a psycho thing?"

"I can give you a couple of examples. A friend wrecked his pick-up. He tried to avoid a street-dog and ran off the road into a drainage ditch and into a tree. He was knocked unconscious, had a few contusions, cracked some ribs, but he dreamed that he was in Lisbon, Portugal, sightseeing with his sister, who was on vacation there. His sister wakes up with an eerie feeling that something had happened to her brother. She calls their mother and receives confirmation."

"Okay, another."

"This guy is mowing his lawn and began thinking about a trip he would make during the following week to close on the sale of property he inherited from his dad. He visualizes an old friend, whom he has not seen in several years. He sees himself in the friend's living room sipping a scotch and water and reminiscing over old times and acquaintances. Suddenly his wife appears at the door as he passes, she makes a signal that he has a phone call. Guess who it is? The friend tells him that he was thinking about him and wondered when he was going to visit. This was the first call that the friend had made to him in twenty years. Coincidental or psychic?"

"I'm about eighty percent skeptical and twenty percent curious."

"But you want to be enlightened. N'est pas, bon amie?"

"Do you see the future or the past or both?"

"Nothing is impossible. In which direction would you like to travel?"

"If I had a choice, I would look at history."

"Good choice, then you could discover confirmation. Tell you what; I'll pick three additional people that I know that have reception and we will take a little trip. You can participate and observe."

"Are you talking about a seance?"

"That would be a good beginning. You have challenged me to open a door. Now do you have the courage to walk through, to meet the challenge?"

"Exactly what are we talking about here?"

"It takes five, because, traditionally, the formation covers the points of a pentagram. The other three, who you will not know, have demonstrated a spiritual influence over destiny. They make things happen. All together, we harness tremendous psychic energy. We are far more sensitive together than apart as individuals. It's called synergistic energy. You will be a dead spot but you will feel a tingling sensation as our energy passes through you. Once you are part of the chain, you cannot break the flow until it's over."

"What if I do?"

Think of it as musical chairs. As long as the music plays, all is well. However, when it stops, there is one seat too few for the participants. One will be left out of the game. As we conjure up a spirit, hopefully, it will reveal itself to us, join us, pass through us, talk through us, and perhaps materialize so we can see it. Breaking the chain, like stopping the music, will add one player more than bodies."

"Wow. Wait a minute. Are you suggesting that somebody

will walk away possessed by a spirit?"

"I didn't want to use those words but that is exactly what would happen. This is why you must make a choice to be in or to be out. There is no in-between ground."

"How dangerous is this?"

It takes a while for a possession to dissipate. Some have to be coaxed out by a medium."

"You mean an exorcism?"

"Well, yes and no. Please remember that spirits on the loose are by nature unsettled or they wouldn't be lingering about. For the most part they are docile. They do harmless things like rattle pots and pan, make chilling breezes; you know stuff like that. They may enter your psyche and attempt to make you act out some behavior like turning stove knobs off and on in the middle of the night. Something that was, important to them while they were among the living. Its just easier to ignore them and get on with living than to get all excited about there being something else that may have sporadic control of your behavior. In the case of the stove-knob ghost, she had left a stove top burner on high causing a fire which consumed her house. I mean there usually is a very logical explanation for their compulsive behavior."

"You mean that I could be found changing baby-doll diapers in the middle of the night, acting out some spook's fantasy?"

"In all probability not, you would be new to the pentax and it would consider you to be a non-contributing force. I wouldn't worry myself about it. The risk is minimal. There is another possibility. Part of the inherent danger of turning on an intensified psychic receiver is that you get what is available. That is to say, we could just as easily attract an evil and destructive spirit. When the first of us senses such an influence, we break off immediately. The potential for damage is minimized. We give it a rest and try again in a few weeks."

"This is pretty scary stuff. When will the next seance be?"

"Tomorrow night."

"Where?"

"We move it from place to place. Eleven o'clock on the parade ground of Fort Moultrie."

Turning his beer bottle bottoms-up, Jack asked, "Can I bring a witness?"

"No. The others won't allow it. You will be there only at my invitation. They will accept you because they know that I have screened and properly prepared you. What we do is not against the law; but, if a rumor started, the clergy would burn us at the stake. Their view hasn't changed much since the middle ages. They sort of feel like they have exclusive dominion over the spirit world. They would take it to the pulpit and play the press against us. Mums the word. We will all know if you talked anyway, so don't embarrass yourself. If you plan to be there, tell Susan you are going to a Lodge meeting and will be home late. If I see you, fine; if I don't, I'll understand."

Each headed for their cars and departed in opposite directions wondering what the following night would bring.

Jack was employed at Tiller Products Company as a sales manager, a job he had kept for three years. The job required very little technical knowledge or experience; in fact, he was the sales department. His brother owned the company and needed somebody to attend conventions, trade shows, and to make yearly field visits to the twenty-five best customers. He was married to a school teacher; they had no children. Jack had no ambition and changed jobs as frequently as his incompetence was discovered. He could talk a good game but had no skill with which to follow through. He was too lazy to really try to take control of his life.

Randy was the opposite in character to Jack, which is probably the reason they were friends. Jack was always relaxed and some of his lackadaisical attitude would loosen up Randy. As a child Randy was hyper-active and precocious. He was always at the top of his class and, as you might expect, attended a prestigious college. At work, he was the typical absent-minded professor whose mind was always in the ozone. At one time he chain smoked claiming that it calmed him down. His field of choice was bio-chemistry; but after nearly thirty years of laboratory work, research, and countless staff meetings, he chose early retirement. Prior to his departure, he sketched out a five year program of research and product development for the company. He continued to check-in once or twice a week. His mind was truly brilliant and moved at lightening speed. He had no attachments. A cook and cleaning lady kept his life orderly from day-to-day. His avocation was chasing reports of ghost sightings, or as he put it, paranormal happenings.

When Jack found his way into the fort with a flashlight as his only defense against the darkness, he immediately saw and waved to a group of people sitting around a candle in the field.

As he got close to the group, Randy said, "Hey Jack. Glad you could make it. Have a seat. We were about to start. I'll make introductions later. Now Jack," Randy continued, "Cross your legs just like us. Let you knees touch the guys on your left and right. Place your hands in your lap. Close your eyes and roll them back like you are about to go to sleep. Concentrate on the flame in the center. Picture it in you mind. Once you are relaxed, let out a cleansing breath. We will all know that you are ready to start."

For about a minute Jack sat as instructed but could only concentrate at how utterly ridiculous all this seemed. He didn't think that anything would happen; but being in the company of three strangers, he felt intimidated at expressing any resistance. The credibility that three other believers brought to the seance added weight to Jack's thought that maybe Randy would make something happen.

Jack could not see their faces. Their heads were bent and covered by caps. Their jacket collars were pulled up to cover the sides of their faces. Their hands were inside their jacket pockets. All Jack could see was nose tips and beard-stubbled chins. Jack amused himself by thinking they were the three monkeys who could see, hear, and speak no evil. Jack pushed his hands into his coat pockets thinking he would be the monkey that would feel no evil.

He asked Randy if he could open his eyes from time to time. Randy instructed him to keep his eyes closed for the time being until he felt confident that the tingling sensation had started and that he might be seeing visions and mental pictures. He told him to really concentrate on finding that spot on his cerebral dial where messages might be received. Jack thought that the only tingling he would feel, would be in his butt from sitting cross-legged on the ground.

He did begin to hear and feel something. There was a sound like leaves rattling, and a moment later he could feel a slight breeze on his face. At first it was warm but as the distant leaves settled, it got cooler and colder and then icy.

Jack blinked his eyes open to glimpse at Randy rocking back and forth like Stevie Wonder and Ray Charles do when they sing to an internal tempo that only they can hear. Randy was trying to translate his tempo into a spiritual presence. Randy began to moan. No words, just a monotone hum without rhythm.

Jack blinked a glimpse again to see that Randy's head was up as though, with eyes still closed, he were star gazing. The other three seemed to have not moved. Randy spoke. "The spirits are with us. They are good. They want ..um..um. No. They want our help..um. They want us to save them..um."

Jack blinked his eyes open and shut again. Randy continued. "Tell me you name..um. Guh..um. Gokhos. Yes. I see you. You lived here. This was your land. These are your people. I see your village. I see your hut. There is a fire smoldering. I smell it's smoke. I see fish drying on a rack above the fireplace."

Jack thought, no he knew, he smelled smoke. Pictures of indians and a village in a piney forest popped into his mind. He didn't know whether they were images pulled from deep recesses of forgotten pages of a National Geographic or fresh from Gokhos through Randy.

Uncontrollably, Jack yelled, "Yes! Yes! I see them. I can

smell the smoke." Jack was beginning to feel the tingling sensation. He could feel the hairs on the back of his neck move. He didn't feel cold any more; in fact, he felt a warmth as though he had just swallowed a shot of Bourbon whiskey. The candle was flickering and popping with excitement. "I see the children, naked running with broken mellon pieces in their dirty hands. I see the dogs following and jumping. They are all yelling and laughing. They are all so happy.

Randy continues, "Gokhos is climbing a tree". He takes his name from the owl who watches by night. He is the village lookout. He watches for men in boats or on foot. Men who will steal the women and who would kill his sons, brothers, uncles, and father if they fought back. From time to time boys of age would wander off from the village. Some would return with a fresh kill to share with his people. Occasionally one would return with a girl that he took from another village. Many never returned. Jack seemed to know all this without asking.

These thoughts just seemed to come naturally into his head like a voice on the radio telling him the rest of the story. Jack tried to concentrate much more intensely. He never used his brain this hard in his life. He could feel the bark between his legs. He could feel his bare feet pushing himself up the tree, climbing to a branch, looking in the forest for a sudden flight of birds as a sign of disturbance. Through Gokhos's eyes he could see the riven from bank to bank.

"Amochol! Amochol!" Jack yells.

Jack stands up in fright waving his arms, shouting, and yelling to the invisible villagers. Jack's contact with the other participants is broken. He has become Gokhos in the flesh. Randy too sees the Spanish Galleon in the river. Both know the soldiers on the huge boat have seen the smoke from the fire.

Jack shouts orders to the village men to get their weapons. He sees lots of men with shiny hats get into smaller boats. There are thirty or forty of them. They have animals larger than forest deer (Achtu) held by strings. The village elders (Kikeyjumhet) and wise man (Kikeyen) dress themselves in ceremonial robes and step to the place that seems to be the landing spot of the visitors to talk peace. All this Jack spoke in excellent tongue of the language only known to Gokhos's villagers and to Randy.

"They are coming! They are coming!" Jack yelled as he shinnied down the coarse black bark of the pine tree. Flakes of bark sheets spiraled in the air causing the dogs to bark, leap, and snap at them as they had done to the children with the melons. The village was in an uproar of confusion. The children were screaming; mothers were calling for them. The older women were gathering possessions of hides, beads, pots, utensils, and body ornaments until they had packs so full and heavy that they could neither lift nor carry them to security. They would defend their life's booty where they stood. Mothers grasped their infants in their arms, grabbed others by hand, some followed their calls as they retreated. Able bodied men took hunting tools as defensive weapons, hid in positions behind trees and bushes, and waited for a signal from the elders that would tell them - friend or foe.

The Spaniards saw that the Indian elders were dressed in colorful bird plumage and had beads made only from shells. They had no metal weapons, gold, or precious stones as ornamentation. These were a poor people. They would make good slaves. The soldiers continued to unload the boats. The first had now returned with empty barrels and the elders of the boat were making signs to fill the barrels with fresh drinking water. They also wanted the smoked fish from above the fire pit. They traded a lance with a metal point. The young men were more curious than cautious of these new people who appeared harmless. Each had to feel the metal and weight of the lance.

The Spaniards laughed and gave the elders a special drink called Rum. The elders laughed and danced like hunters. The drink had the power to make them young

66

again. The young men were amazed and drew closer to the medicine of the big-boat and heavy-hat people with big deer they could ride. Full of powerful medicine, the elders rode the deer. There was great rejoicing in the village as great fires were built and all ate from the food stores of the villagers. They danced. The women and children returned to watch from the shadows the foolishness of their elder men.

The Spaniards could hear the giggling of the women in the distance. The forty Spaniards had not seen a woman in three months. The village men were filled with drink and were only capable of stumbling in a confused token of resistance.

"Hellam! Hellam!" (Run! Run!) Jack screamed as he stumbled and fell onto two of the mute seance participants. Gokhos took a lance deep into his chest. It was a mortal wound and made Jack writhe with pain. He died on the parade ground of Fort Moultrie.

The next morning his cold body was removed by the EMS to the county morgue for Susan to identify.

Two days later at the mortuary there was a very touching service for Jack. He had apparently died of a massive heart attack. No one could figure out why he was in the fort with a stub of a candle in his hand.

Randy joined the line of mourners to pay respects and condolences to the grieving widow.

As he embraced Susan, he whispered softly in her ear, "Will I see you tonight?"

"Yes"

"Usual place?"

"Yes, I miss you."